Text copyright © 2013 by Dianne Ochiltree
Illustrations copyright © 2013 by Betsy Snyder
All rights reserved/CIP data is available.
Published in the United States 2013 by
Blue Apple Books, 515 Valley Street,
Maplewood, NJ 07040
www.blueapplebooks.com
First Edition
Printed in China  08/13
ISBN: 978-1-60905-291-1
2 3 4 5 6 7 8 9 10

Dianne Ochiltree

# It's a Firefly Night

art by
**Betsy Snyder**

BLUE APPLE

When the moon is high
and the stars are bright,

Daddy tells me,
"It's a *firefly* night!"

I hop off the porch.
I feel the air
warming my legs
and messing my hair.

Grass tickles my toes.
I zip through the yard,
chasing fireflies—*gotcha!*—
to put in my jar.

Fireflies shimmer.

One, two, **three, four, five**.
My jar's like a lightbulb
that's just come alive.

Fireflies glimmer.
All of them glow.
I race to show Daddy
their dancing-light show.

Flickering quicker,
they sparkle and shine.
I love catching fireflies,
but they are not mine.

I take one gently
out of the jar.
My hand is a cage
for one tiny star.

Uncurling my hand,
easy and slow,
I whisper good-bye,
then I let it go!

Soon many fireflies
open their wings.
They flitter and flutter,
soar over my swings.

Ten, nine, eight, seven, six—
drift through moonlight.
Five, four, three, two, one—
blink in the night.

We walk back to the house.
I hold Daddy's hand tight.
"Will tomorrow," I ask,
"be a firefly night?"

On hot summer days,
fireflies rest in tall grass or on
the leaves of plants and trees.
They like to fly around between
dusk and midnight when the
air is damp and cool.

Although
commonly called
a "firefly" or "lightning
bug," this insect is
really a beetle.

Fireflies
range in size from
1/5 inch to one inch
in length.

Fireflies
need moist habitats.
They are found around
swampy and grassy areas,
often at the edge of creeks,
streams, and ponds.

The firefly grows in stages, from egg to larva to adult insect. Some larvae give off light. When that happens, people call them "glowworms."

Scientists believe fireflies light up in rhythmic patterns to attract mates or to warn one another about dangers.

Farmers and gardeners love fireflies because the larvae eat many snails, slugs, and other pests.

Because they live only three to four weeks, most adult fireflies do not eat. A female firefly will lay up to five hundred eggs on the underside of leaves, in moss, or in water.

There are over two thousand firefly species.